THE TROUBLE WITH
TYRANNOSAURUS REX

Written and illustrated by Lorinda Bryan Cauley

Harcourt Brace & Company

SAN DIEGO   NEW YORK   LONDON

For my sons,
Ryan and Mack

Library of Congress Cataloging-in-Publication Data
Cauley, Lorinda Bryan.
The trouble with Tyrannosaurus Rex.
Summary: Ankylosaurus and Duckbill devise a plan
with the other peaceful dinosaurs in their neighborhood
to outwit and humiliate Tyrannosaurus Rex
before he eats them all.
[1. Tyrannosaurus rex — Fiction..2. Dinosaurs — Fiction]
I. Title.
PZ7.C2746Tr   1988   [E]   86-33637
ISBN 0-15-290880-3
ISBN 0-15-290881-1 (pbk.)

B C D E
D E (pbk.)

Printed in Singapore

The illustrations in this book were done in colored pencils on Fabriano paper.

The text type was set in Meridien by Thompson Type, San Diego, California.

The display type was set in Albertus by Thompson Type, San Diego, California.

Printed and bound by Tien Wah Press, Singapore

Designed by Michael Farmer

Production supervision by Warren Wallerstein and Eileen McGlone

STORYTELLER'S NOTE

I decided to write this book especially for my sons, Ryan and Mack, whose intense curiosity and interest in dinosaurs made me want to learn more about these prehistoric animals. My sons had collected as many factual dinosaur books as they could, but they longed for a story where dinosaurs were the main characters—an imaginative story with dinosaurs who were almost human, as animals often are in fairy tales and fables.

Some of Ryan and Mack's favorite dinosaurs lived in the Cretaceous period, so I chose this as a setting and have tried to be as accurate in visual details as possible. Since the exact colorations and skin textures of many dinosaurs are still unknown, artists can only piece together the available facts and guess the rest. There are many unsolved mysteries about dinosaurs—and that may be one of the reasons we find them so interesting today.

LONG AGO, when dinosaurs ruled the earth, there was one particularly hungry Tyrannosaurus Rex who was determined to gobble up all the other dinosaurs in the neighborhood.

It got so bad that the littlest dinosaurs would scarcely come out of hiding, even for a drink of water. And the more Tyrannosaurus Rex scared his neighbors, the louder he bragged, the more he strutted, and the better he thought of himself.

In that same neighborhood, two young dinosaur friends named Duckbill and Ankylosaurus lived close to each other on the banks of a clear lake.

One morning when Tyrannosaurus Rex was off raising dust someplace else, the friends were quietly munching plants and sharing their daydreams while they basked in the warm sun.

"Ah, this is lovely," sighed Ankylosaurus. "We should do this every day."

"But you know if we didn't take care we'd be mid-morning snacks for you-know-who," Duckbill replied.

"Our very own neighborhood tyrant," sighed Ankylosaurus.

Duckbill smiled. "Perhaps not for long," he said slyly.

"What are you talking about?" Ankylosaurus asked. "He could eat ten of me and ten of you and *still* be hungry."

"Just so," said Duckbill, gathering courage. "His stomach is ten times larger than his brain. His arms are too short, and he's as clumsy as they come."

"But he's good at eating dinosaurs," Ankylosaurus said.

"Exactly. So if we gather everybody here for a party by the lake this afternoon, he's sure to show, right?" said Duckbill.

"For an early supper," sighed Ankylosaurus.

"Okay, then let me tell you my plan. . . ."

That afternoon, the dinosaurs pretended to have a party. Almost everyone in the neighborhood came. There was a tasty feast of leaves, pinecones, and magnolias. Triceratops led the games, and everyone had a grand time.

For about five minutes.

Then suddenly the ground shook. Twigs snapped, leaves crunched, and fear filled the air.

Some two-legged dinosaurs scurried by.

"He's coming! He's coming!" they shouted, frantic in their hurry to get to a nearby cave.

Everyone scattered. Even the horned dinosaurs in the field stopped grazing and scooted into the brush.

Duckbill took cover behind a tree.

Only Ankylosaurus stayed where he was. This was part of the plan. As it happened, he was also too scared to move.

All at once Tyrannosaurus Rex appeared, crashing through a
grove of trees. His sharp teeth glistened in the afternoon light.
''I do believe I've found a snack,'' he cried.

In a few great strides, the towering beast was above Ankylosaurus, ready to sink his teeth into the creature below him. He snarled and cackled while Ankylosaurus shook with fear.

"W-w-wait!" cried the smaller dinosaur. "Look over there! That nice soft Duckbill would make a m-m-much better lunch than me. M-m-more fleshy! No horns, like me. Eat him!"

The hungry beast took one look at Duckbill and roared. His enormous jaws trembled greedily, and he lunged toward this new treat.

All he saw was Duckbill—a fine, fleshy meal. He didn't see Ankylosaurus, who was creeping up behind him.

Wham! With a forceful swing of his tail, Ankylosaurus knocked the huge clumsy creature off balance.

He toppled into the lake with a gigantic *kersplash!*

Angrier and fiercer than ever, Tyrannosaurus Rex struggled out of the water. Dripping wet, he screamed and plunged directly at little Ankylosaurus.

Just as Tyrannosaurus Rex was about to seize his friend, Duckbill used his tail to hurl a glob of mud into the monster's eyes.

Tyrannosaurus Rex tried to wipe the mud away, but his tiny arms were useless. For the moment, he couldn't see a thing!

Hearing the cheers and chuckles of Duckbill and Ankylosaurus, the other dinosaurs carefully crept out of hiding. Before long, they surrounded the helpless beast, whispering nervously among themselves.

Tyrannosaurus Rex was tantalized by the smells and sounds of so many dinosaurs—so many meals—this close to him. He rushed furiously but blindly from one voice to the next, spinning around and around and around . . .

. . . until finally, in dizziness, he crashed to the ground.

The other dinosaurs gathered close around him in disbelief.

"Now what?" they all asked. "When he wakes up, he'll be a bigger bully than ever."

Duckbill only smiled. "Wait and see, wait and see," he said. "The trouble with Tyrannosaurus Rex is that he's only happy when he's the boss. I don't think he'll stick around too long after this."

That night, the dinosaurs had a real party—a grand celebration. There was feasting and dinosaur dancing that lasted far into the night.

And sure enough, when nobody was watching, Tyrannosaurus Rex quietly slunk off into the woods—never to be seen in that neighborhood again.

As for Duckbill and Ankylosaurus, they lived a long and serene life along the banks of the clear lake, munching plants and sharing their daydreams while they basked in the warm sun.

Pteranodon
(ter-AN-oh-don)

Anatosaurus (the "duckbill")
(an-AT-oh-SAW-rus)

Saurolophus
(SAWR-oh-loaf-us)

Tyrannosaurus Rex
(tie-RAN-oh-SAW-rus REX)

Corythosaurus
(ko-RITH-oh-SAW-rus)

Styracosaurus
(STY-rak-oh-SAW-rus)

Triceratops
(try-SER-a-tops)

Dromaeosaurus
(DROME-ee-oh-SAW-rus)

Pachycephalosaurus
(PAK-ee-SEF-al-oh-SAW-rus)

Ankylosaurus
(an-KY-low-SAW-rus)

Struthiomimus
(STROOTH-ee-oh-MIME-us)